The Noisy Way to Bed

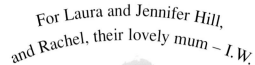

For Laura and Jennifer Hill,
and Rachel, their lovely mum ~ I. W.

For Joshua and Amélie,
with happy memories of room 303 – T.B.

First published 2003 by Macmillan Children's Books
This edition published 2004 by Macmillan Children's Books
a division of Macmillan Publishers Limited
20 New Wharf Road, London N1 9RR
Basingstoke and Oxford
Associated companies throughout the world
www.panmacmillan.com

ISBN 978-0-333-98673-8

Text copyright © Ian Whybrow 2003
Illustrations copyright © Tiphanie Beeke 2003
Moral rights asserted.

5 7 9 8 6

A CIP catalogue record for this book is available from the British Library.

Printed in China

The Noisy Way to Bed

Ian Whybrow

Illustrated by Tiphanie Beeke

MACMILLAN CHILDREN'S BOOKS

It's bedtime!

This little boy was ever so tired
And this is what he said:
"I think I'll go home past the pond,

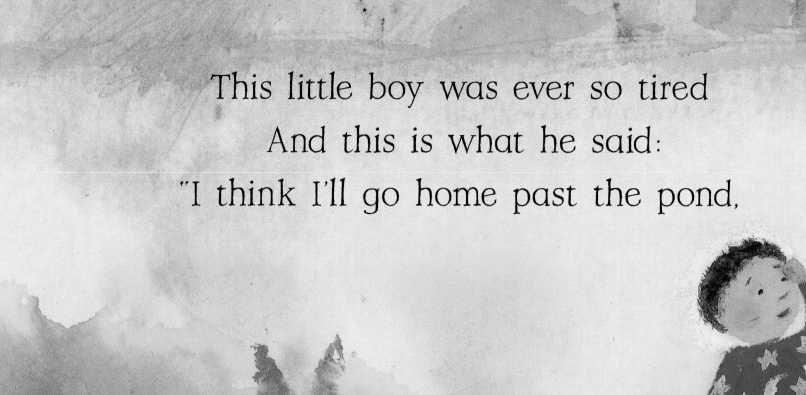

Because this is the way to ..."

"Quack!"

"Oh no! This is not the way.
I'd better go another way instead."

A sleepy boy and a sleepy duck
Go waddling past the shed.
Through the gate and under the tree.

This is the way to . . .

"Oh no! It must be across the field."

A sleepy boy and a duck and a horse
Gently go ahead.
Over the field, past the sheep.

This is the way to . . .

"Sorry to bump into you, Mrs Sheep.
Do you know where our bed is?"

A boy, a duck, a horse, a sheep,
Look carefully where they tread.
They tiptoe past the pigsty.

This is the way to . . .

"Oink!"

"Oh, sorry to make you jump, Mr Piggy.
We're very tired, too.
Will you help us find our bed?"

Five sleepy creatures found the stairs
And followed where they led.

"Neigh!" "Quack!"

"Oink!" "Baaa!"

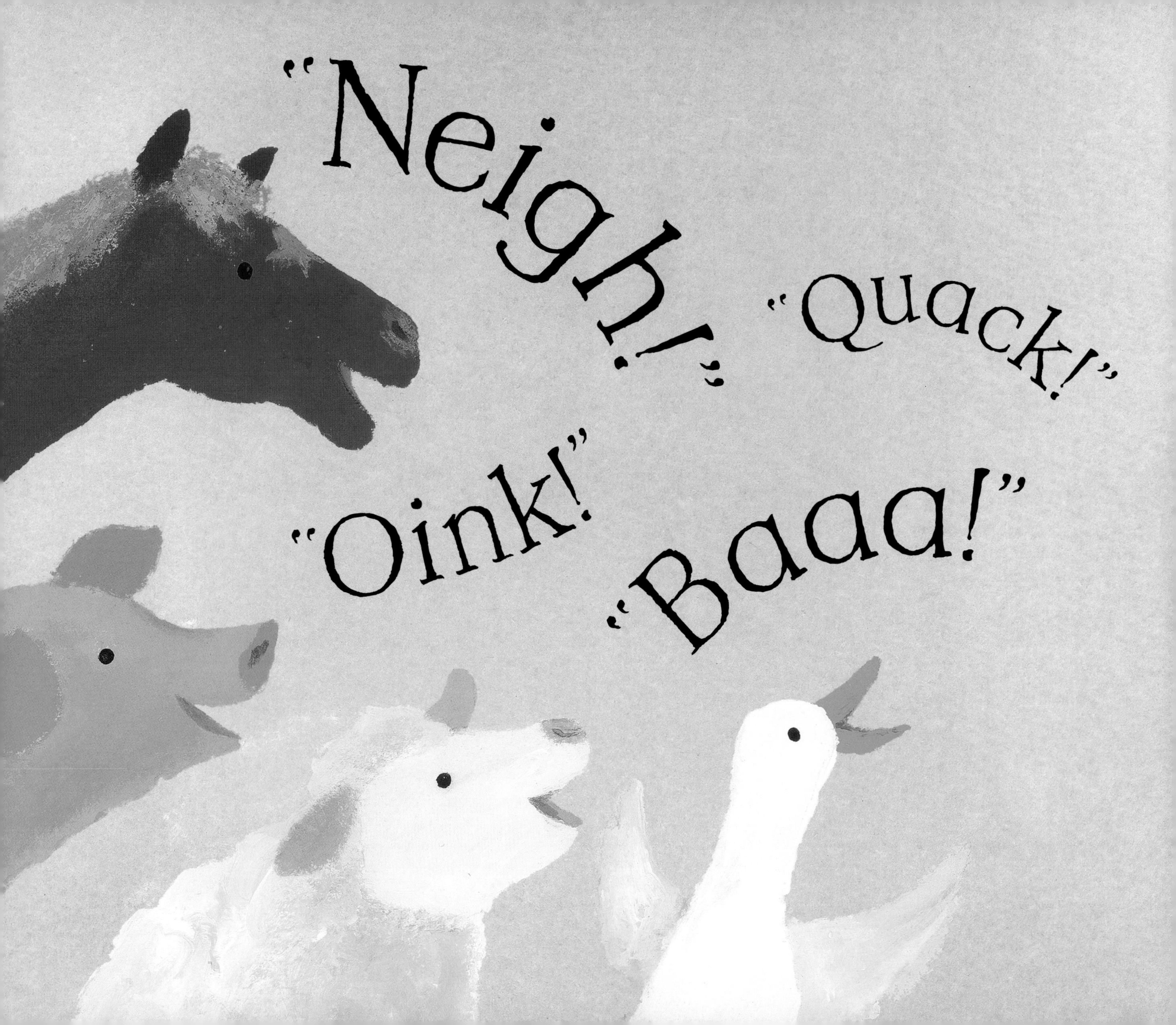

And the sleepy little boy said,

"Quiet!
Shhhhhhh!"

What a noisy way to . . .

bed!